For my sister, Pauline

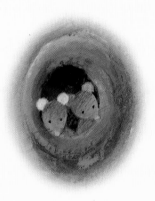

ORCHARD BOOKS
96 Leonard Street, London EC2A 4XD
Orchard Books Australia
32/45-51 Huntley Street, Alexandria, NSW 2015
This edition produced for The Book People Ltd
Hall Wood Avenue, Haydock, St Helens WA11 9UL
ISBN 1 84362 386 2
First published in Great Britain in 2003
Text and illustrations © Tony Maddox 2003
The right of Tony Maddox to be identified as
the author and illustrator of this work
has been asserted by him in accordance with
the Copyright, Designs and Patents Act, 1988.
A CIP catalogue record for this book is
available from the British Library.
1 3 5 7 9 10 8 6 4 2
Printed in Dubai

Not so loud, Oliver!

Tony Maddox

TED SMART

It was night-time
on Mulberry Farm.
Time to sleep for all
the baby animals.

Everywhere was
still and quiet.

The cows were snoring softly in the barn.

The chicks were cuddled up cosily in the henhouse

and the ducklings were dreaming gently amongst the reeds.

Too-Wit Too-Woo!

But high up in the
roof of the oldest barn,
Oliver Owl wasn't sleepy.
He stretched his wings and
gave a loud, "Too-wit, Too-woo!"

"MOO!" called Mamma Cow from below.

"Shhh, not so loud Oliver! My little calves are sleeping."

Oliver practised being quieter.
In the softest of soft
voices he sang,

Too-Wit
Too-Woo!

"Cluck! Cluck!"
called Mamma
Hen from the
henhouse.

"Shhh, not so loud Oliver!
It's my little chicks' bedtime."

So Oliver tried one last time. In the smallest of small voices he whispered,

Too-Wit Too-Woo!

"Quack, quack!"
called Mamma Duck
from the duckpond.

"Shhh, not so loud Oliver!
My little ducklings are sleepy."

Oliver gave a sigh,
and flew up, up, up to
the branches of his favourite
oak tree. There he sat silently
while the farmyard animals
slept down below.

But what was that dark
shape creep, creep, creeping
towards the henhouse?

It was Foxy Fox,
and he was
looking for his
evening meal!

Closer and closer he crept,

past the duckpond, around the barn

and right up to the henhouse door.

Oliver had to do something
– and quick! He flapped
his wings as fast
as he could . . .

It was so loud that it
woke Mamma Cow
who started to "MOO!"

It was so loud that it woke Mamma Hen who started to

"Cluck!"

And it was so loud that it woke Mamma Duck who started to

"Quack!"

Oliver's voice was
so loud that it scared
Foxy Fox right away.

And from then on, nobody minded Oliver's singing . . .

Too-Wit
Too-Woo!

Well, not much!